BALLPARK Mysteries 19

THE BLACK CAT CHANGE-UP

BALLPARK MYSTERIES®

Also by David A. Kelly

Babe Ruth and the Baseball Curse

BALLPARK
Mysteries 19

THE BLACK CAT CHANGE-UP

by David A. Kelly

illustrated by Mark Meyers

Curveball Books Boston

This book is dedicated to my Black Cat mystery team: Mark Meyers, who found new ways to bring Kate and Mike to life with his wonderful illustrations for this book (and the preceding 22 Ballpark Mysteries books); Jen Arena, who helped me sharpen the story, action, and dialogue; Jon Ford for his copyediting expertise; and Oliver Nash, who went above and beyond when it came time to turn my manuscript into a polished and published product. I, and the readers, thank you!
–D.A.K.

To Mike and Kate (and David of course), what a blast it has been to venture across the country and work through so many mysteries together!
–M.M.

"The Mets have shown me more ways to lose than I even knew existed."
–Casey Stengel, NY Mets manager 1962–65

Text copyright © 2022 by David A. Kelly
Cover art and interior illustrations copyright © 2022 by Mark Meyers

All rights reserved. Published in the United States by Curveball Books, Boston.

Ballpark Mysteries® is a registered trademark of Upside Research, Inc.
Ballpark Mysteries Logo © Penguin Random House LLC
Disclaimer: This Ballpark Mysteries book is not published by Penguin Random House LLC

Visit author David A. Kelly on the web at: davidakellybooks.com

School and library author visits available at dakvisits.com

Library of Congress Control Number: 2022916542
Library of Congress Cataloging-in-Publication Data
Names: Kelly, David A., author. | Meyers, Mark, illustrator.
Title: The Black Cat Change-Up / by David A. Kelly; illustrated by Mark Meyers.
Description: First edition. | Boston: Curveball Books, 2022. | Series: Ballpark mysteries; 19 | Summary: Cousins Mike and Kate investigate when the ghost of the 1969 Mets black cat threatens to disrupt an important game between the New York Mets and the Chicago Cubs at the Mets ballpark.
Identifiers: 978-1-9593-7800-6 (trade) | 978-1-9593-7802-0 (ebook) | 978-1-9593-7801-3 (lib. bdg.)
Subjects: |CYAC: Baseball—Fiction. | New York Mets (Baseball team)—Fiction. | Mystery and detective stories. | New York—Fiction. | Cousins—Fiction. | Baseball stories. | Cousins—Juvenile fiction. | History. | LCGFT: Detective and mystery fiction. | Ghosts—Fiction.

Printed in the United States of America

Swing for the fences!

Contents

A Bad Omen

"No, no!" Mike Walsh yelled. He sat up in his sleeping bag on the floor. The New York City hotel room was dark and quiet.

Mike's cousin, Kate Hopkins, clicked on the light. She had been asleep in the sofa bed next to him. "What happened?" she asked. "Are you okay?"

Mike swiveled his head to look around the room. He rubbed his sleepy eyes.

"It was awful!" he said. "I had a night-

1

mare that Mr. Met was chasing me! He said my head looked funny. He wanted to turn it into a baseball!"

Mr. Met was the mascot for the New York Mets baseball team. He had a huge baseball head perched on the shoulders of a regular-size body. Mr. Met and his wife, Mrs. Met, were popular sights at the Mets' stadium. Mike had bought a Mr. Met pillow earlier that day while he and Kate were sightseeing in New York City. Kate's mom was taking them to a Mets game the next day.

"Well, there's one good thing about having a baseball head," Kate said. "If you carried around a baseball bat, you could get a hit anytime you wanted!"

"That's not funny!" Mike threw his Mr. Met pillow at her.

Kate ducked. The pillow bounced off the wall and landed on the sofa bed.

"I'm done with him!" Mike said as he flopped back down on his sleeping bag.

Kate dropped an extra pillow onto Mike's stomach.

"Ooof!" Mike said. "Hey! I'm trying to sleep here!"

* * * * *

"You need to wake up, sleepyheads, so we can get our day started," Kate's mother called out at nine the next morning. "First up, sightseeing. Then, this afternoon, we're going to meet Cookie Clifford before the game. He's the Mets' second baseman and star hitter. He agreed to say hello to you since you're both big baseball fans!"

"That's great!" Kate said.

3

Mrs. Hopkins was a sports reporter. Kate and Mike often joined her when she traveled to different ballparks. Today she was covering that day's game between the Mets and the Chicago Cubs. It was an important game. Whichever team won would advance to the National League playoffs and possibly the World Series.

Mike groaned and rolled over. "I'm only getting up if you promise we won't run into Mr. Met!" he said into his pillow.

"Come on, 'fraidy cat!" Kate said. "We won't let him chase you. Besides, Mr. Met is sure better than Mettle the Mule."

Mike poked his head up. "*What* the Mule?" he asked.

Kate pulled him out of his sleeping bag by his arm. "Mettle the Mule," she said. "I read about it in the Mets history

book on the way here." Kate loved to read and always had books with her. "Mettle was the Mets mascot for a few years in the 1970s. He lived in a pen in the right field of Shea Stadium, near the Mets' bullpen."

"What happened to him?" Mike asked.

"1979!" Kate said. "After the Mets lost ninety-nine games and came in last place, they ditched Mettle to see if it would help."

"Did it?" Mike asked.

"Sure," Kate said as she twirled strands of her brown hair through her fingers. "They only lost ninety-five games and came in second to last in 1980!"

Mike groaned and slid back down onto his sleeping bag. "I don't want to see Mettle the Mule or Mr. Met!" he said.

After breakfast, Mike, Kate, and Mrs. Hopkins visited the Empire State Building and the New York Public Library. They ate a late lunch near Grand Central Terminal, then jumped on a number 7 subway train, which took them directly to the Mets–Willets Point station just outside the Mets' stadium.

"There's the Home Run Apple from Shea Stadium, the Mets' old ballpark!" Kate said. A large red apple on what looked like an upside-down black hat stood in front of the stadium entrance. "The apple used to rise up out of the hat every time the Mets hit a home run!"

Kate's mom took a picture of Kate and Mike in front of the Home Run Apple. Then they crossed the concrete plaza to the main gates. People were starting to gather for the big game.

Mrs. Hopkins showed her press pass to the security guard at the gate and he waved them through. They stepped into the Jackie Robinson Rotunda, a large circular area with escalators to the upper levels. On the ground level was the entrance to the Mets Hall of Fame and a gift shop.

Mike spun around to take it all in. "Why so much Jackie Robinson stuff?" he asked. Large pictures of Jackie Robinson flanked either side of the stairs to the upper level. "He played for the Dodgers, not the Mets!"

"The Mets wanted to honor both the Dodgers and Jackie Robinson," Kate said. "The Dodgers with Jackie Robinson played in New York before they moved to California. And they're a National League team, just like the Mets."

Kate twirled to see all the words etched into the stone above the rotunda archways. *Courage, Excellence, Persistence, Justice, Teamwork, Commitment, Citizenship, Determination,* and *Integrity.* "Those are Jackie Robinson's core values," she said. "I read about them in the Mets history book."

"Look at that giant number 42!" Mike said. Two huge blue numbers dominated the space under the escalators. Each was as tall as a person.

"Forty-two was Jackie Robinson's number," Kate said.

"Even I know that!" Mike said.

Mike raced Kate toward the 4 and 2, but before they got there, a man in a Chicago Cubs hat stepped out from between the giant numbers.

"Louie Lopez!" Mike called out.

"¡*Hola*! Mike and Kate!" Louie said. "My two favorite detectives. I was hoping I'd see you here!"

Louie was the star center fielder for the Chicago Cubs. Mike and Kate had helped him solve a mystery during the World Series. Louie gave them each a high five. He tipped his hat at Mrs. Hopkins as she joined them.

"It's great to see you again," Kate said.

9

"Excited for today's game? It should be a good one!"

Louie smiled and nodded. He flexed one of his arms and pointed to it. "I feel good about the game. We're strong," he said. "But I don't think the Mets are feeling so good about it now, especially the superstitious players!"

Mike and Kate looked at each other.

"What do you mean?" Kate asked.

"Didn't you hear about the ghost of the black cat?" Louie asked. "It's haunting the Mets!"

Cookie on the Run!

"A ghost that's a cat?" Mike asked. "You've got to be *kitten* me!"

Louie Lopez shook his head. "I'm not. And it's no joke for the Mets," he said. "I heard some of the players are pretty rattled."

"Why would a black cat bother them?" Mrs. Hopkins asked.

"A lot of baseball players are super superstitious," Louie said. "Like if they're

11

on a hitting streak, they don't want to shave. Or they don't wash their jerseys when they're winning. It can be anything in this game. You never know what's going to give you good luck. Or bad!"

"Don't forget the 1969 Cubs versus Mets game," Kate said to her mother. "The Cubs were leading in the National League East and the Mets were behind by a game and a half. In the fourth inning a black cat ran onto the field near the Cubs' on-deck circle! It scampered past the Cubs' dugout and disappeared. The Cubs lost the game by six runs and eventually lost the division to the Mets, too. The Mets went on to win the World Series that year!"

"Exactly!" Louie said. "Now a black cat, or the ghost of 1969's black cat, is jinxing the Mets. I'm okay with that.

We need to win this game!"

"I guess what *ghost* around comes around," Mike said as he nudged Kate. She just rolled her eyes at him.

"What's the ghost done?" Kate asked.

"Well, no one's seen the ghost or an actual cat yet," Louie said. "But Mudcat Lee, the Mets catcher, and Pablo Rogers, their shortstop, both got threatening phone calls two days ago. The only thing the caller said was 'Watch out! The black cat is coming back for the Mets!'"

"*¡Eso da miedo!*" Kate said. She was learning Spanish and knew that Louie spoke Spanish. "That is scary!"

Louie smiled at Kate. "*Sí*," he agreed. "And after we got here yesterday morning, someone drew chalk pictures of black cats on some doors around the stadium!"

"Wow," Mike said. "Someone's really out to get the Mets!"

Mrs. Hopkins checked her watch. "It was nice to see you, Louie," she said, "but we have to dash. We're scheduled to meet up with Cookie Clifford."

"Maybe I'll see you later, then," Louie said. "I'm heading to the batting cage to get some swings in. I don't want Cookie to beat me to a home run tonight! If you have time, stop by the visitors' batting cage and say hi." Louie turned and walked toward the main part of the stadium.

"I hope Cookie doesn't mind if we're a few minutes late," Mrs. Hopkins said. "It's a big stadium!"

14

Mike, Kate, and Mrs. Hopkins wound through the hallways and past a security guard to the lower level. The stadium was starting to fill up with workers and food vendors getting ready for the game.

Mrs. Hopkins stopped in front of two large brown doors. An orange-and-blue sign above the doors read NEW YORK METS CLUBHOUSE.

"Cookie said to meet him here," she said.

While they waited, Mike tossed a baseball from one hand to the other. He had brought it for Cookie to autograph.

"There you are!" A short, stocky man stepped up to them. "I'm Cookie," he said. "You must be Mrs. Hopkins. And this must be Kate and Mike. Nice to meet you!"

Cookie noticed Mike's ball. "Want me to autograph that for you?"

With a grin, Mike handed the ball over.

15

Cookie pulled a marker out of his pocket, signed the ball on the sweet spot, and gave it back to Mike.

"Now, how'd you like to see the Mets' locker room?" Cookie asked.

"We'd love to," Kate said.

"Great!" Cookie said. "Come on in!" He opened the clubhouse doors and led them down a carpeted hallway. At the end was the locker room, a long and wide space with lots of comfortable sofas and chairs. Carpet covered the floor, and deep lockers lined the side walls.

"This is great!" Mike said as he took it all in.

"It sure is," Cookie said. "Follow me. I'll show you my locker." They passed one locker after another until Cookie stopped in front of one with his name in orange letters across the top.

"I can't wait to . . . to . . . to . . . Hey, what's that?" Cookie pointed to a black cloth covering a box on the shelf at the bottom of his locker.

Mike peeked under the cloth. He smiled. "It looks like a special gift for you, Cookie."

As he stood back up, Mike pulled the cloth off the box.

Underneath was a cat carrier. A cute furry face smiled out at them.

"It's a cat!" Mike said.

Kate crouched down for a closer look.

But Cookie didn't. He stared blankly at

the cat for a moment. Then he took a step back and held his hands out in front of him. He made a soft sputtering sound.

"Ca . . . Ca . . . Ca . . . ," he struggled to say.

And then, all of a sudden, Cookie dashed out of the locker room!

A Black Cat
on the Loose

"Cookie!" Kate called.

Mike and Kate ran after him. Mike pushed the locker room door open, and he and Kate popped out into the hallway.

"Cookie, it's okay!" Mike yelled. "It's just a cat!"

Cookie had run halfway down the empty hallway. When he heard Mike, he stopped and turned around and leaned against the concrete wall. He waved Kate and Mike off as they approached.

"Thanks, but I'm fine," he panted. "It's nothing to worry about!"

Kate and Mike glanced at each other. "Um, are you sure?" Kate asked. "You seemed pretty surprised."

Cookie took a deep breath and straightened up. A small smile crossed his face. He shrugged sheepishly.

"I guess now you know my secret," he said.

"What?" Mike asked. "That you keep animals in your locker?"

Cookie shook his head and scuffed at the ground with his blue-and-orange sneaker. "No," he said quietly. "That I'm afraid of cats!"

"You mean lions and tigers?" Mike asked.

"No," Cookie said. "Well, I don't like those, either. But I mean cats. Like pet cats. Like the one in my locker!"

"Oh," Mike said. "We get that. Kate's afraid of bagpipes and I'm afraid of robots."

"Cats unsettle me," Cookie said. "Something about the way they're always swiping at things with their paws. And the

way they pounce. It just isn't normal. And on top of that, black cats bring bad luck!"

Kate nodded. "Louie Lopez told us about the ghost of the black cat," she said.

"That doesn't sound good."

"It's not!" Cookie said. "We've got a tough game coming up, and if we have bad luck, we won't make the playoffs! I can't be near anything that might throw off my hitting, especially tonight. We need to win."

"I'm pretty sure that the cat in your locker is okay," Mike said. "Let me show you!"

Mike tugged on Cookie's shirt and led him back to the locker room. Mrs. Hopkins was still in front of the cat carrier. A cat's face peeked out from behind the grates of the carrier door.

Mike opened the cat carrier and reached inside. He pulled out a gray tabby cat and held it up in front of Cookie.

"Don't worry, it's okay!" Mike said. "It's a stuffy! Like a teddy bear! It's not a real cat at all. There's nothing to be afraid of."

Cookie let out a big sigh. "Oh," he said as he nodded. "That's good! That's very good. I don't mind stuffed cats!"

Mike tossed the toy to Cookie.

"It's kind of soft." Cookie cuddled the stuffed cat and rubbed its head.

Just then, the clubhouse door opened

and someone came inside, whistling.

"There he is!" the tall bald man with a black mustache crowed. "Cookie the Cleaner! The best cleanup hitter in the league! At least that's what all the Mets fans are talking about when they should be talking about me, the best pitcher on the team! You know, everyone on the team can hit, but only a few are pitchers. We're the ones who win the games, not you!"

When the man noticed the stuffed cat, he stopped.

"Aw, how cute!" he said. "But I thought you didn't like cats."

Cookie shrugged. "I don't," he said as he petted the toy. "But maybe this one is okay. Mike, Kate, Mrs. Hopkins, this is Sanford Sims, our star pitcher. He's a nice guy, but a little jealous of all my fans."

"Nice to meet you," Sanford said. He had a deep, gravelly voice. "Cookie, are you planning on playing today? Bob the security guard saw you running down the hallway a few minutes ago. He said you seemed upset. Maybe you should take a few days off to rest."

Cookie stopped petting the cat. He studied Sanford and rocked back on his heels. "Is that what this is about?" Cookie asked. "Did you try to scare me by putting this cat in my locker so I'd take a few days off?"

Sanford smiled and winked at Mike and Kate. "Maybe a few days off would help you relax! You could take your new friend to visit

some big cats in the Bronx Zoo, like the lions and tigers! I can take care of winning tonight from the mound."

"Not a chance," Cookie said. "Cats or no cats, I'm shutting down the Cubs tonight with my hitting. They'll be the ones with bad luck."

Sanford let out a deep rumbling laugh. "We agree that the Cubs will lose, even if we don't agree on why," he said. "But now it's time for me to get ready for the game." Sanford put his hat on and headed to the other side of the locker room.

"Sanford doesn't seem to like you much," Kate said quietly.

"My fans are the best and he's jealous," Cookie said. "They call themselves the Cookie Crew and show up to cheer me on. He wishes his fans were as loud as mine!"

Cookie set the toy cat down in his locker.

"Thanks for the help with the cat." He glanced at the clock. "I have to go work on my swing. Maybe we can meet up later."

"No problem," Kate said.

They followed Cookie to the clubhouse's main door. Mike, Kate, and Mrs. Hopkins only made it a few steps down the hallway when they heard Cookie cry out.

They spun around. He was standing in front of the clubhouse door with a piece of paper in his hand.

"What's wrong?" Mike asked.

"This was taped to the door!" Cookie said.

He handed Kate the piece of paper.

Watch Out, Mets!
The Black Cat Is Coming to Tonight's Game!
But This Time It's Coming for You!
—The Ghost of the Black Cat

The Cat Sneak

"This is awful!" Cookie slumped against the clubhouse door. "First a phone call about a ghost, then the chalk drawings, and now a threatening note!"

Kate handed the note to Mike, and he examined the message. It was written in black marker on a plain piece of paper. He folded it and slipped it into his pocket.

"You got a call about the ghost, too?" Kate asked. "I thought only Mudcat and Pablo did!"

Cookie straightened up a little. "Yes, two days ago," he said. "I didn't tell anyone else because I didn't want to spook the team. I was home helping my daughter build a rocket for her class project. My phone rang. A deep voice said the Mets should watch out—the ghost of the black cat was coming back for us! Then the caller hung up. No phone number showed up on my caller ID, so I couldn't report it."

"Was it Sanford?" Mike asked. "Maybe he's trying to get you to take a game off so he can take credit for the Mets winning."

"Naaah," Cookie said. "Sanford is jealous of my fans. And he does like to play practical jokes. But he wouldn't mess up an important game like this, that's for sure. Our whole team knows how much we need to win this game."

"We'll help you figure this out," Kate said. "Mike and I are pretty good detectives. For now, forget the ghost of the black cat and focus on the game."

"That would be great," Cookie said. "If you need anything, just ask. You can let people know you're helping me. I'll be at our batting cage."

Mike gave Cookie a fist bump. "We're going to watch Louie Lopez at the Cubs' batting cage, but we'll see you later," he said.

With a tip of his cap, Cookie disappeared into the clubhouse.

"Well, I've got to get to work." Mrs. Hopkins handed Kate and Mike two tickets for their seats and some money. "Check in with me a little later and enjoy the game!" She waved goodbye and started for the press box.

"We've got to find a way to help Cookie," Mike said.

"Right," Kate said. "Let's check if Louie has learned anything else about the ghost. And then we can ask security if they saw anyone bring the cat carrier in!"

Mike and Kate ran through the stadium hallways until they reached the visitors' batting cages, which were near the visitors' clubhouse. An athletic-looking teenage girl in a Cubs baseball hat stood outside the door. She had long blonde hair tied back in a ponytail. She glanced at Mike and Kate as they approached.

"Can I help you?" she asked.

"Maybe. We're looking for Louie Lopez," Mike said. "We saw him earlier, and he said he'd be taking some swings in here. Are you with the team?"

"Kind of," the girl said. "I was a bat girl last year, but I'm not this year. They brought me along so I could see this game. I'm helping out the equipment manager if he needs it."

"Cool!" Kate said. "I always thought it would be neat to be a bat girl. How did you get the job?"

"My grandpa used to work for the team, so I had a connection," the girl said.

"Did you get to travel with the team last year when they did road trips?" Mike asked.

The girl shook her head. "No," she said. "Batboys and girls don't travel with the teams. Instead, the teams just bring along a huge duffel bag filled with uniforms of all sizes. They lend one to the home team's batboy or bat girl to wear!"

"I'd love that job," Mike said. "Maybe they'd let me keep the baseball caps from all the different teams. Then I'd have a huge hat collection!"

The girl smiled. "I did it a bunch of times last year for the visiting teams. I ended up with six or seven different hats, which was great!"

Mike held his right hand up and gave the girl a high five. "Way to go! My name's Mike Walsh and this is my cousin Kate Hopkins. We're from Cooperstown."

"I'm Ash Santo." The girl stood up

straight. "Nice to meet you. What do you need Louie for?"

"We're trying to solve the mystery of the ghost of the black cat," Kate said. "Some strange things have been happening."

"Oh, yeah. Phone calls and drawings of cats on doors?" Ash said. "That sounds spooky. Louie Lopez told me it had something to do with a game in 1969 and bad luck, but I'd never heard of it before. Has something new happened?"

"Yes," Kate said. "Someone left a cat carrier in Cookie Clifford's locker. The stuffed cat inside freaked him out. We wanted to ask Louie if he had heard anything new and check with security to see if they noticed anyone with a cat carrier earlier today."

"Oh, cool," Ash said. "But you don't have to do that!"

Mike and Kate stared at Ash. She twirled a few strands of her long blonde hair around her fingers while she waited for Mike or Kate to respond.

"What do you mean?" Kate asked. "We need to find out who's messing with Cookie before the big game."

"You don't have to talk to security," Ash said. "Because I know who did it!"

The Black Cat's Ghost, Caught?

"You do?" Mike asked. "You know who's causing the cat trouble?"

Ash nodded.

"Who?" Kate asked.

Ash leaned back against the wall. "Well, I don't know his name," she said. "But when I came to the stadium early today to help set up the equipment, I saw one of the Mets players just ahead of me. He had a cat carrier in his left hand!"

"He did? What did he look like?"
Mike asked.

Ash held her hand up high in the air.
"Tall, about six foot three, maybe," she
said. "Bald head and a black mustache."

"Sanford!" Mike and Kate both said at
the same time.

"He's the Mets' pitcher," Kate said. "We

saw him in the locker room earlier. He didn't seem to like Cookie much."

"And he's got a deep voice," Mike said. "Like the caller that Cookie described!"

"That sounds like him," Ash said. "I think he's your guy!"

"I can see why he might have played a practical joke on Cookie," Mike said, "but why would he draw black cats on doors? Or make threatening calls about the ghost of the black cat?"

"Maybe to rattle Cookie," Kate said. "It doesn't matter why he did it. We should tell Cookie!"

"What about checking in with Louie?" Mike asked Kate.

"Oh, he was here earlier," Ash said. "But he's busy with a trainer at the moment and can't be disturbed."

Mike nodded. "Okay. Thanks for the info, Ash. We'll go find Cookie. See you later!"

"Good luck catching Sanford," Ash said. "I guess you never know who to trust anymore!"

As Mike and Kate headed back down the hallway, the sounds of the fans streaming into the stadium echoed from the level above them. Mike checked his watch. "It's batting practice time," he said. "The Mets will be up first. That means Cookie should be on the field waiting his turn. Let's go!"

Kate and Mike ran through the stadium and bounded down the aisle between home plate and the Mets' dugout. A short wall stood between them and all the players waiting their turn at bat on the field. Clusters of fans were sprinkled throughout the stadium, hoping to catch balls or get signatures from players.

A Mets player was taking practice swings at home plate. A coach stood on the pitcher's mound behind a screen, getting ready to pitch again. Fielders hovered in the infield and outfield, waiting for hits.

"That's him!" Kate pointed to the batter at home plate. "Cookie's up."

The coach pitched one ball after another. Even though they were easy pitches, Cookie's swings were all over the place.

He swung late on one ball.

And early on another.

He hit a dribbler down the first-base line.

And a pop-up directly to the pitcher.

Not one ball in ten made it out of the infield.

It looked more like a bad T-ball practice than a warm-up before a major-league game.

Kate covered her eyes. "Oh no," she said. "He's terrible today!"

Unlike Kate, Mike couldn't take his eyes off Cookie. "It's so bad that it's almost good," he said. "It's like when I was trying to hit every ball like a home run. I just kept whiffing!"

Finally, Cookie's turn was over. He pulled off his batting helmet and headed to the far side of the dugout. His shoulders slumped, and he dragged the bat along the ground behind him.

"Cookie!" Kate and Mike called out. "Over here!" They waved to catch his attention.

Cookie glanced sideways. A small smile crossed his face when he saw them. He picked the bat up and motioned for Mike and Kate to meet him on the far side of the dugout, away from his teammates.

"I sure hope you didn't see that," Cookie said when he

reached the wall. A black safety net stretched up above the wall to stop foul balls. "I was awful! All this stuff about black cats and ghosts has me rattled. This is going to be a tough game."

Kate bounced on her toes and thumped the infield wall with her palm. "That's what we came to tell you," she said. "We might have found out who's causing the cat trouble!"

Cookie's eyebrows lifted. "Really?" he asked. "Who?"

"Sanford!" Mike said.

"We just talked with a girl who's helping out the Cubs," Kate said. "She saw Sanford walk into the stadium with a cat carrier! He snuck it in before the rest of you were there!"

"It's definitely the kind of practical

joke that Sanford would play on me," Cookie agreed. "If it's him, that explains a lot. Good work!"

Cookie smiled for a moment, then it faded. "But that doesn't explain the ghost of the black cat," he said.

"It might," Kate said. "If Sanford left the cat for you, he could have been the one who drew the cats in the stadium yesterday."

"And called you and the other players on the phone," Mike said. "You said the caller had a deep voice. Sanford's voice is deep and gravelly."

Cookie let out a sigh. His shoulders slumped again. "I hope you're not right, but it seems like you might be," he said. "It all fits. I guess the Mets have a traitor in our clubhouse!"

A Chorus of Cats

"What are you going to do?" Kate asked.

"I've got to go investigate," Cookie said. "If Sanford is trying to make us lose, I'll put a stop to it!" He picked up his bat, slung it over his shoulder, and started for the dugout.

"Check in with me later. I'll let you know what happens!" he called back.

Mike leaned against the infield wall as Cookie walked away. He rubbed his belly.

"As much as I'd like to get something to eat," he said, "I think we need to keep investigating until Sanford confesses or we can prove that he did it!"

"I agree," Kate said.

"Let's review the evidence so far. We have strange phone calls to some Mets players, the cat drawings in the stadium, and the note on the clubhouse door. Anything else?"

"Not yet," Mike said. "But let's double check that note for clues." He pulled the note out of his back pocket and opened it. They both read it.

"That means something is going to happen during tonight's game," Kate said.

"Maybe it'll be a black cat again," Mike said. "Like in the 1969 game. Someone is going to put a cat onto the field!"

"If a black cat is going to spook the Mets tonight, it will probably have to show up near their dugout," Kate said.

"But it will have to get through this!" Mike took a step back from the infield wall and glanced up. Black safety netting to prevent foul balls from hitting fans ran all the way from behind home plate to near first and third base.

Kate tried to slip her hand through

the netting. It didn't fit. "A cat can't get past that!" she said.

"I know," Mike said. Then he made climbing motions with his arms while he took pretend steps up. "But what if the cat climbs up and over the netting!"

"No cat would do that," Kate said. She followed the netting along the wall in the direction of the outfield. "Maybe there's a break that a cat could get through."

A few sections of seats later, the wall of netting ended.

"You could put a cat on the field here," Kate said. "But it's too far away from the dugout. The cat might go for the outfield."

Mike started back the way they had come. "Let's check in the other direction."

They walked back along the netting until just before they reached the Mets' dugout and Mike stopped. "The photographers' area!" he said. "That's it!"

At the end of one of the aisles near the dugout was the photographers' area. There was a break in netting above the low concrete wall on one side. It was the one place near the infield without netting!

"A cat could definitely get onto the field here . . ." Kate's voice trailed off.

On the other side of the Mets' dugout, fans who had been watching batting practice burst out laughing. Out on the field, Cookie and some of the other Mets were pointing to the home-plate side of the dugout in surprise.

Mike tapped Kate on the shoulder. "Come on!" he said. "Something's happening."

They zigzagged past empty seats to the group of fans on the other side of the

dugout and skidded to a halt.

"Oh, hi again," a voice said.

Mike and Kate glanced to their left. It was Ash.

"What's going on?" Kate asked.

Ash held a finger up to her lips. "Shhh!" she whispered. "Just listen!"

Mike and Kate looked at each other

. . . and then they heard it.

MEOW!

MEOW!

MEOW!

MEOW! MEOW!

MEOW! MEOW! MEOW!

MEOW!

It sounded like a chorus of cats . . . in the Mets' dugout!

On the Prowl
for the Original

"The Mets are being attacked by cats!" Ash said. "Can you believe it?"

One cat meowed after another.

MEOW! MEOW! MEOW!

More and more fans crowded toward the dugout. Two security guards ran over from the outfield.

"I don't see any cats!" Kate said. "Are they inside?"

"I hear them!" Mike said. "They must

be here somewhere!"

Ash shrugged. "Someone said it's the ghost of the black cat coming back for the Mets!"

One of the security guards disappeared into the dugout. He ran back a few moments later with a big orange plastic drink cooler. He took off its top and dumped gallons of orange drink on the ground. Then he and the other security guard started scooping up small white plastic disks from in front of the dugout. They tossed them into the cooler.

The meowing grew louder and louder!

Finally, one of the guards put the cooler's lid back on.

Suddenly, it was quiet.

The meows had stopped.

The guard stood up. He waved his arms as if to shoo the fans away.

"Okay, okay," he said. "You can all return to batting practice. We're finished herding the cats!" He opened the cooler, reached in, slipped the lid back on, and held up one of the disks for the crowd to see.

MEOW!

"Seems like we have a practical joker at the game today," he said. "Someone put cat-sound prank toys all around the dugout. But I'll bet Mr. Met didn't think that was funny! You don't want to get on the bad side of Mr. Met. He's got a pretty big head, and he's not afraid to use it!"

The crowd laughed and started to drift away.

"Any idea what happened before the meows?" Mike asked Ash.

Ash shook her head. "Nope. I was just down here watching batting practice and waiting for the Cubs when I heard some funny sounds," she said. "At first it was just one or two meows. Then it got louder and louder!"

"Did you see the Mets pitcher, Sanford, around?" Kate asked. "Or anyone who looked suspicious?"

"Um . . ." Ash twirled some strands of her hair around her finger as she thought. Her hair was pulled back in a ponytail held by an elastic with two bright white-and-red baseballs. "I didn't see Sanford. But now that you ask, there was an older guy with a Yankees hat near the seats on the far side of the dugout. He left just before all the meows started!"

"What did he look like?" Mike asked.

"Hmmm," Ash said. "He was shorter. Gray hair. Looked like a grandfather. Blue jacket with a Yankees hat."

"Thanks," Kate said. "That's helpful. I guess it makes sense that a Yankees fan could be behind this. The Mets and Yankees are big rivals."

"Well, I don't know that he was responsible," Ash said. "But it might be worth checking out."

Mike scanned the stadium walkways. "I don't see him anywhere," he said. "But we should go look. Sometimes criminals hang around the scene of the crime because they like the excitement!"

"Sure," Ash said. "See ya!"

Mike and Kate bounded up the stairs to the main level. It was getting close to game time, so the walkway was filling up with Mets fans in blue-and-orange shirts, caps, and jackets.

By the time Kate and Mike had made two complete trips looking for the suspicious Yankees fan, batting practice had ended. The grounds crew was raking the base paths and painting the baselines. The stadium was almost full of fans, excited for the big game.

Mike and Kate stopped by a food stand overlooking the field. Mike leaned on the metal railing. He kicked at the cement floor with his sneaker.

"Nothing!" he said. "We've seen Cubs fans, Red Sox fans, and even Padres fans!

But no Yankees fans that look like the guy that Ash spotted."

"Maybe it was a disguise," Kate said. "Maybe he looks completely different or something. We have to keep thinking."

"Thinking?" Mike sniffed the air. "I'm definitely thinking all right. I'm thinking I'm hungry!" He straightened up. "Popcorn? Hot dogs? Pretzels? I'm thinking, what should I pick? A bit of food would help us figure out the black cat mystery! Let's eat!"

"Good idea," Kate said.

Mike was so hungry, he finished one hot dog on the way to their seats. But luckily, he had bought two. He started on the second as they sat down. Their seats were right behind the Mets' dugout, on the aisle. The photographers' area was just ahead of them.

Kate munched on her tacos as Sanford headed to the mound to start the game. The crowd went wild. Their cheering continued to build until he threw the first pitch.

As the ball crossed the plate, the Cubs batter swung with a hard, chopping motion.

WAP!

The ball sailed far over the first baseman's head!

"Oh no!" Mike called, forgetting his hot dog for a few moments.

The batter dropped the bat and ran for first. Then he started for second. The ball flew on and on until it finally cleared the right-field wall.

It was a home run for Chicago!

The crowd went quiet.

It was going to be a long game for Mets fans.

Right from the start, the Mets didn't play well at all. They seemed rattled. One fielder after another made errors by missing catches or throws, letting Cubs runners on base. The Mets finally got three outs from the Cubs, but it wasn't pretty. The Cubs ended the top of the inning four runs ahead.

"Looks like the ghost of the black cat scared the Mets!" Mike said as the Mets got ready to bat.

AT BAT		BALL			STRIKE
	1	2	3	4	5	6
CHI. CUBS	4					
N.Y. METS	0					

Kate nodded. "That type of play isn't going to get anyone into the Hall of Fame, that's for sure."

Mike slapped the armrest of his seat. "That's it!" he said. "The Hall of Fame!"

"The Baseball Hall of Fame in Cooperstown?" Kate asked.

"No!" Mike said. "You just gave me an idea where to look next. If we're looking for the ghost of the black cat, maybe we should start by investigating the real black cat!"

"What do you mean?" Kate asked.

"We need to learn more about what happened with the original black cat in 1969!" Mike said. "Maybe there's something we're missing."

He stood up and pointed in the direction of the Jackie Robinson Rotunda. "Let's see if the black cat game is in the Mets Hall of Fame!"

The Ghost Arrives

The Mets Hall of Fame was mostly empty when Mike and Kate arrived. A few fans lingered in front of plaques highlighting famous Mets players. Exhibits on the stadium and team history lined the walls. In the back was an entrance to the Mets gift shop.

"Oh no!" Mike cried as he walked through the entrance door. "There's Mr. Met!"

Mike made a show of ducking behind a display case and covering his head.

"After that dream I had, I don't want him anywhere near me," he said to Kate. "He'll probably try to ram a big baseball head on my shoulders!"

Kate tugged her cousin's arm. "Come on. It's just a mannequin." She pulled Mike over to the life-size model dressed in a Mets uniform with a huge smiling baseball head.

Mike stared at the Mr. Met mannequin. "I don't know," he said. "You can't trust Mr. Met. He's sneaky!"

Mr. Met didn't move.

Mike smiled. "All right. I'm not going to let you scare me anymore." He opened and closed his hand in front of Mr. Met's face. "Because if you come near me, I'll get a giant glove and snap it shut on your head! We'll see how much you like that!"

Kate laughed. "And maybe we'll get a giant tub of Lena Blackburne Baseball Rubbing Mud and cover him in it!"

"Yeah!" Mike said. "We'll muddy you up!"

He gave Kate a high five.

"Okay," Kate said. "Enough of Mr. Met. Let's see if we can find a black cat."

Mike and Kate ran from one exhibit to another, searching for information on the original black cat. They spotted huge gold World Series trophies from 1969 and 1986 and examples of the different uniforms the Mets had worn. There was also an exhibit on the Polo Grounds and Shea Stadium, two stadiums where the Mets used to play.

Mike spun on his heels as he scanned the room. "Where's the black cat?" he asked.

They had explored almost every part of the museum. "What about that display in the corner?" Kate asked.

They skidded to a stop in front of a small display.

"Bingo!" Mike said.

A big black-and-white photo showed a Chicago Cubs batboy holding a bat, a Cubs player in the on-deck circle, and a long line of Cubs players sitting on the bench in their dugout.

But it was the middle of the picture that caught Kate's eye.

A black cat stood on the dirt, facing the Cubs players on the bench. It looked like it was just about to pounce!

Below the picture, there was a short description. It read:

Kate read the description out loud. She looked for more details in the exhibit, but there weren't any.

Mike sighed. "We already know most of that," he said.

"We didn't know the final score or the on-deck batter's name," Kate said. "The name of the batter from Chicago sounds familiar to me. Ron Santo. Is he famous?"

Mike shrugged. "Sort of," he said. "He played for the Cubs for a long time, and he's in the National Baseball Hall of Fame. But he did do one thing that's a little quirky. He was known for jumping and clicking his heels together when running home."

"That's funny," Kate said.

"It was until it wasn't," Mike said. "Santo stopped doing it on September 2, 1969, a week before the black cat game. The Cubs were in first place and won the game that day. But they had a complete collapse after that. Some people said they started losing because Santo stopped the heel clicks. But others said it was the black cat at the Mets game!"

"I guess it could be either," Kate said. Sho tapped the glass of the display case. "I think we've found out all we can here. We should get back to the game. Maybe the Mets' luck has changed!"

Mike and Kate ran back to their seats. It was the bottom of the second inning and the Mets were batting. They had three men on base but two outs. The Cubs were ahead 4 to 0. But the Mets fans were on their feet, going crazy. A home run now would tie the game!

"Look! Cookie's up at bat!" Kate said.

The Cookie Crew chanted Cookie's name loudly as the pitcher threw the ball.

It was right over the plate.

Cookie swung hard.

SWISH!

He missed! Strike one.

The pitcher threw two more pitches. Both were balls. The count was two balls, one strike. The Mets runners on base were raring to go.

Cookie swung at the next pitch.

He missed for a second time!

The count was two balls, two strikes.

Mike and Kate jumped up and cheered.

"Let's go, Mets!" they shouted. The noise in the stadium was deafening.

Cookie took some practice swings and waited for the pitch.

The Cubs pitcher hurled the ball.

It flew right for the catcher.

Cookie swung big as it crossed the plate.

WAP!

The ball popped into the catcher's mitt.

Cookie struck out!

The crowd groaned and booed. The second inning was over. The Mets were still losing.

"That's bad!" Mike said as he slumped down into his seat.

"I know," Kate said. "I think the ghost of the black cat has arrived!"

A Cat Connection

Before the Mets took the field for the start of the third inning, Cookie scanned the crowd. When he spotted Mike and Kate, he waved for them to meet him down at the infield wall.

Mike and Kate ran down the steps.

"What's up?" Kate asked.

"I wanted to let you know that it's *not* Sanford," Cookie said. "Even though he put the cat in my locker, I know for a fact that he's not causing the other problems."

"How?" Mike asked.

"Easy!" Cookie said. "After I thought more about your suspicion, I realized I was playing golf with him yesterday when the drawings of the black cat appeared in the stadium. Neither one of us was anywhere near there, so he can't be the one behind the ghost of the black cat.

That means someone else is out to get us tonight!"

"I guess it's good the Mets don't have a troublemaker on the team," Mike said. "But it doesn't help us find the criminal."

Cookie pounded his fist into his open baseball glove. "I know," he said. "But we've got you two on the case! Let me know if you come up with any other ideas about the black cat!"

Cookie turned and ran out to second base. Mike and Kate returned to their seats.

"Now what?" Kate asked.

"I've got an idea," Mike said. "What if there was a clue in that exhibit? I had forgotten about Ron Santo until I saw the display. What if he's causing the trouble?"

"That was a long time ago," Kate said. "Why would he be trying to scare players with the black cat now?"

"Revenge!" Mike said. "Remember, some people blamed the Cubs' failure on Santo for stopping his heel clicks. But others blamed it on the black cat walking by him when he was in the on-deck circle. What if Ron is somehow trying to get back at the Mets for the bad luck the Cubs had after the black cat?"

"Hmm, could be," Kate said. "Maybe he traveled here with the team."

Mike stood up. "Exactly," he said. "And I know where we can find out. The Cubs' clubhouse!"

Kate and Mike ran through the stadium hallways to the Cubs' locker room entrance.

"Hold up there!" a guard said, stopping them. "This room is off-limits."

"I'm Mike and this is my cousin Kate,"

Mike said. "We're friends with Louie Lopez, but we have a question for you."

"Me?" the guard asked. "What can I help you with?"

"Is there any chance that Ron Santo from the 1969 Cubs is traveling with the team?" Mike asked.

The guard immediately shook his head "No, definitely not," he said. "I'm afraid Mr. Santo died a few years back."

"Oh, sorry to hear that," Kate said.

The guard nodded.

"Well, thanks for letting us know," Mike said.

He and Kate headed back down the hallway. Once they were out of earshot of the guard, Kate sighed. "That didn't work," she said.

"No, but maybe it was the right idea," Mike said.

"What do you mean?" Kate asked. "It can't be Ron Santo!"

"Right!" Mike said. "But it could be another Cubs fan! We were looking for a Yankees fan because Ash said that's who she saw near the dugout. But what if she was wrong? What if we should be looking for a Cubs fan? Like, maybe it's a friend or something of Ron Santo," Mike said. "Or just a big Cubs fan. Or a Cubs fan trying to get revenge for 1969."

Kate stopped suddenly.

"That's it!" she said. "Good catch!"

Mike spun around. "What's it?" he asked. "What did I say?"

"What if the person we're looking for was present when everything happened?" Kate asked. "Like they were here in the stadium the day the pictures of the black cat were drawn. And they were near the dugout when the cat toys were put out. And they had access to players' phone numbers. And they were a Cubs fan. And, most importantly, they had a reason to get revenge."

"Yes!" Mike said. "That's *exactly* who we need to find."

"Maybe not," Kate said. "We might already know who it is!"

Mike stared at Kate. "We do?" he asked.

"Ash!" Kate said. "Ash *Santo*!"

"Ash? Santo?" Mike said.

"Ash said her last name was Santo when we met her," Kate said. "Maybe Ron was her grandfather or uncle. She said her grandfather worked for the team!"

"But she was so nice to us," Mike said.

"And the Yankee fan was a red herring! She probably made that up trying to mislead us," Kate went on. "I'll bet she put out those cat-noise makers herself. She was right by the dugout when it happened."

Kate turned and headed back to the guard. He raised one eyebrow at them. "Back again?" he asked.

"Yes," Kate said. "But now we're looking for Ash Santo. Is she around?"

"Nope," the guard said. "I haven't seen her in hours."

"Oh, okay," Kate said. "Hey, do you know if she's related to Ron Santo?"

"She sure is! Ron was her grandfather," the guard said. "That's why she's here for this game. She asked if she could come along."

"Interesting," Mike said. "She told us she was helping out the equipment manager."

"Oh no," the guard said. "Our equipment manager doesn't let anyone help him. Ash is just here for luck."

"Any idea where we can find her?" Kate asked.

The guard scratched his head. "Nope," he said after a few seconds. "Maybe she's watching the game."

"Okay, thanks," Mike said.

"That proves it!" Kate whispered as they walked away.

"How?" Mike asked.

"Ash lied to us!" Kate said. "She told us she'd never heard of the black cat game. But she knows all about it! We've got to find her before she jinxes *this* game!"

The Cat Arrives

The main level of Mets' stadium was filled with fans finding their seats or heading for food. It was the bottom of the fourth inning. The Cubs were still ahead 4 to 0.

"Ash has got to be here somewhere," Mike said. "Let's start near the dugout. We can circle the stadium until we spot her."

But Ash wasn't anywhere near the Mets' dugout. Nor the outfield. Nor any of the other sections around the stadium that Kate and Mike searched. Even after splitting up to scan the hallways and seating areas, the cousins came up empty.

"It's like she disappeared," Kate said as she dropped into her seat.

"But she couldn't have," Mike said, still looking around. "We know she's up to something. We just have to figure out where she might show up!"

"Well, if the black cat is going to mess with the Mets, it will probably be near their dugout," Kate said, gesturing to it a few rows ahead of their seats. "We've got a good view from here."

Mike nodded. "I'll watch the field and the game," he said. "You keep an eye on the stands."

The Mets were still behind, but at least they had stopped the Cubs from getting any more runs that inning. The Mets right fielder, Gopher Murphy, was up at bat. The count was three balls and no strikes. The crowd was on its feet cheering for a hit.

Mike stood up, stamped his feet, and whooped for the Mets.

The Cubs pitcher let a fastball fly.

Gopher saw his opportunity.

He swung down hard and fast.

THWAP!

The ball exploded off the bat and rocketed for the outfield!

Gopher dropped the bat and ran for first as a wave of

cheers rolled through the stadium.

The ball sailed over the second baseman's head. It had just cleared the outfield wall for a home run when Mike felt Kate bump his leg.

"Mike! Look at that!" Kate said through the cheering.

She pointed to a figure walking down the steps next to their seats.

It was Mr. Met!

"What's up with Mr. Met?" Mike asked. "He looks a little strange."

Mike was right. The Mr. Met coming down the stairs didn't look like the one he and Kate had seen in the Hall of Fame.

This Mr. Met's head was smaller. It looked misshapen. A black bag hung over his shoulder.

"Why does he have that backpack?" Kate asked.

"More importantly, why is he wearing a Yankees jersey?" Mike asked.

Mike was right. Mr. Met was wearing a Yankees pinstripe jersey, blue jeans, and white sneakers with red stripes on the side. "Is he really a Yankees fan?" he asked.

Before Mike or Kate could say anything else, Mr. Met breezed by them to the small wall separating the end of the aisle from the photographers' area. When he reached the wall, Mr. Met slipped the backpack off and placed it on the wall.

With the crowd distracted watching Gopher circle the bases for his home run, Mr. Met made his move. In one quick motion, he unzipped the backpack, flipped it open, and ran back up the stairs.

The fans were still cheering as Gopher crossed home plate. No one paid attention to the fleeing Mr. Met or what was happening at the wall.

Except Mike and Kate.

"Look!" Kate said. Something had just popped out of the backpack.

It was a black cat!

An Elastic Clue

The cat lifted its tail and arched its furry back high in the air.

Mike jumped into action. "Quick! Grab it before it gets onto the field!" he said. "I'll stop Mr. Met!"

And just like that, Mike was gone.

Kate sprang down the few steps to the infield wall. She scooped up the black cat before it could leap into the Mets' dugout.

"I got you!" she said. Kate cuddled the

cat in her arms. It licked her hand and curled up.

Grabbing the empty backpack, Kate ran up the stairs as quickly as she could with the cat. At the top, she spotted Mike far down tho hallway. He was just turning right into one of the stadium's many stairways.

Kate took off after him, dodging fans left and right.

A moment later, she turned the corner to the stairway.

Mike was just coming down the stairs. He shook his head.

"Mr. Met disappeared," he said. "There's no sign of him on the stairway or the next level. I don't know where he went."

Kate handed Mr. Met's backpack to Mike while she rubbed the cat's head to keep it calm. "Well, he left this little guy behind," she said. "I think we should call him Spooky. Maybe there are clues in that bag."

Mike turned the backpack inside out, but it was completely empty. "Nope, nothing here," he said. "But he could have dropped something as he ran. Let's look."

They scanned the steps.

But they came up empty.

Mike and Kate were about to return to the main hallway when Mike stopped suddenly. He crouched next to the end of the metal stairway railing. Something white was wedged into the space between the railing and the wall at the bottom of the steps.

"What's this?" He reached between the metal slats of the railing. He pulled out a Yankees jersey and a white, rubbery Halloween mask.

"Aha!" Mike said as he shook out the mask. A deflated Mr. Met head stared back at them!

"We found him!" Mike said. "I was worried that Mr. Met was going to make me lose my head. But I guess we made him lose *his* head!"

"Unfortunately, we need more than

that to solve this mystery," Kate said.

When Mike turned the mask inside out to check for tags, something dropped to the ground. "Well, well, well," he said, picking up something small. "I guess it wasn't Mr. Met at all that dropped that cat off near the dugout!"

Kate looked at the object in Mike's hand.

It was two small plastic baseballs with red stripes. And they were on the end of a hair elastic.

"That's Ash's!" Kate said.

A Trail of Clues

"We were right. Ash is the black cat villain!" Mike said.

"And I know how to find her," Kate said. "She's going to want to know what happened to the cat. I'll bet she comes back to take a look. Criminals usually return to the scene of the crime."

Mike stroked the cat's head gently. "What about Spooky?" he asked. "I'm not sure we can go around chasing criminals carrying a cat!"

Kate smiled. "I've got the perfect place for him." With one hand, Kate opened the pocket on the front of her sweatshirt. With her other hand, she guided the cat inside. "Here you go, Spooky!" she whispered. "Here's a nice place to snuggle." She stuffed the Yankees jersey in the other side of the pocket.

Spooky glanced at Mike and Kate. He let out a big yawn and uncurled his tongue. Then he licked his right paw once and burrowed into the comfy front pocket of Kate's sweatshirt.

"There!" she said. "I think Spooky will

be all set for a while. Or at least long enough for us to catch a criminal!"

The game was in the sixth inning by the time Mike and Kate made it to the Mets' dugout. They split up and each went down an aisle on the opposite sides of the dugout. They pretended to look for their seats while keeping an eye out for Ash.

The Mets were still behind by three runs. They had just taken the field. Sanford was on the mound throwing some warmup pitches. Cookie was standing near second base, but he seemed distracted. He kept scanning the stands and taking off his cap to scratch his head.

A few fans were trying to get a Mets cheer going when Kate heard a sharp whistle cut through the air. She glanced over to Mike.

He was looking at Kate and motioning wildly at a figure near the top of his aisle.

It was Ash!

She wore a gray fleece. Her long blonde hair was loose under a Cubs baseball cap.

Kate gave Mike a thumbs-up, cradled Spooky in her pocket, and ran up her aisle. Mike took off up his.

Standing at the edge of the main walk-

way, Ash was staring down at the dugout and scanning the field. Mike and Kate approached her from opposite sides.

"Hello, Ash," Kate said when they were close enough.

Ash turned. She seemed surprised to see Mike and Kate. "Oh, um, hello," she said. She put her hands in her pockets. "Did you have any luck finding the old man in the Yankees jersey?"

"Not exactly," Mike said. "But we found something even better!"

"What?" Ash asked.

"This!" Kate pulled out the Yankees jersey and held it up in front of Ash.

Ash's eyes widened. "So, you did find him!" she said. "I knew it!"

"Well, we found that jersey," Mike said. "But it didn't belong to an old man, like you said. Because we also found this!"

Mike pulled the Mr. Met mask from his pocket.

"Where'd you get that?" Ash asked.

"From a mysterious Mr. Met who tried to put a black cat on the field," Mike said. "To mess up their game tonight!"

"Oh, so you caught him," Ash said. "That's good! I don't know who would want to do that."

"You don't, Ash?" Kate asked.

"Um, no," Ash said.

"That's funny," Mike said. "Because we *know* you did it!"

"What?" Ash asked.

"*You* were wearing this mask!" Kate said. "*You* were Mr. Met with the black cat!"

Ash took a couple of steps back. "I don't know what you're talking about," she said. Her eyes shifted to the left. "I've never seen that mask."

Mike held up the elastic with plastic

baseballs on it. "We found this inside the mask. It must have come off when you took off the mask. We saw you wearing it earlier today."

"We know Ron Santo was your grandfather," Kate said. "You lied to us when you said you'd never heard of the famous black cat game he was in. You're here to get revenge on the Mets. The guard at the Cubs' locker room told us you're not working with the equipment manager."

Ash covered her eyes with her hands.

She slumped back against the wall.

"You're right," she said. "It was me. I'm so sorry."

Mr. Met's Miracle

"Why did you do it?" Mike asked.

Ash scuffed at the ground with her sneaker. She sighed. "At first, I was thinking I could get revenge on the Mets and give them their own bad luck, just like the Cubs got from the black cat in 1969," she said.

"But there was another reason?" Kate asked.

Ash nodded. "The more I thought about the idea, the more I missed my grandfa ther," she said. "I decided this might be a good way to get him some new recognition. A second black cat game would put him in the headlines again. And maybe this time, the Cubs would win!"

As she mentioned her grandfather, Ash took a shaky breath and wiped away a small tear. "I guess it wasn't really the right thing to do," she said quietly.

"No, it wasn't," Mike said. "And it wasn't fair to the Mets players."

"Or the memory of your grandfather," Kate added.

Ash lowered

her head. "I know that now," she said.

"How did you do it? How did you change your voice?" Mike asked. "The Mets players said they got phone calls from someone with a deep voice."

"I used an app on my phone for that," Ash admitted.

"Where'd you get the cat?" Kate asked.

Ash shrugged. "From a nearby rescue shelter," she said. "I picked it up yesterday after we came in. I hid it in the back of a closet in the visitors' locker room. I wasn't going to hurt it. I was just using it to scare the Mets."

Kate patted her front sweatshirt pocket. A soft purr escaped from it. "Well, Spooky's okay," she said. "Lucky for the Mets—and maybe you—Mike and I rescued him before he could scare anybody."

Ash stood up straight and smiled. "I'm glad he's okay," she said. "He seems like a nice cat. I'm sorry I got him tangled up in this. I guess I messed up big-time. I hope they don't put me in jail!"

Kate laughed. "For drawing some pictures and making phone calls?" she asked. "The police have bigger things to worry about."

"I guess you're right," Ash said. "But I still need to face up to what I've done. I'm going to confess to the team. I'll go wait for them back at the clubhouse. I won't go anywhere else—I promise. And this time I'm telling the truth!"

Ash patted Spooky's head through the material of Kate's pocket and headed off in the direction of the Cubs' locker room.

Another contented purr filtered out

into the hallway air. "I'm glad someone's happy," Mike said as he patted Spooky through Kate's sweatshirt pocket. "But I'll bet Cookie isn't. We've got to give him an update before it's too late!"

Mike and Kate ran down the aisle to the infield wall. By leaning over the railing of the photographers' section, they could see into the Mets' dugout.

"There's Cookie!" Mike said. He and Kate waved and called out his name. A moment later, Cookie turned and spotted them. They motioned frantically for him to come over. Cookie nodded. Then he said something to one of his teammates and headed toward them.

"What's so urgent?" he asked as he stepped up to the other side of the short railing. He was still wearing his fielding glove. "We're struggling out there! Every-one is worried about that black cat stuff!"

"We solved the mystery of the black cat!" Mike said. "The cat drawings and the phone calls were done by Ash Santo. She's a Cubs fan and the granddaughter of Ron Santo. She wanted to get revenge on the Mets for the 1969 black cat game."

"But we stopped her before she could cause any more problems," Kate said. "She's in the Cubs' locker room. You should have security talk with her."

A broad smile crossed Cookie's face. He gave Mike and Kate a loud high five with his ungloved hand.

"Really?" he said. "That's great news! Now I won't worry anymore. We'll just play the game!"

Kate's front sweatshirt pocket rustled.

Then a furry black head popped out and stared at Cookie.

"What's that?" Cookie took a quick step backward and bumped into a camera stand. "What's going on?"

"It's okay," Kate said. "He won't hurt you!" She scooped Spooky out of her front pocket and held the cat up. "This is Spooky! Ash was going to release him on the field during the game to bring bad luck to the Mets, but we stopped her."

Cookie took a step forward. He slowly held out his hand. Spooky licked one paw and eyed Cookie. Then he sprang!

"Wait!" Cookie cried.

But it was too late!

Spooky flew through the air. Cookie hold out his glove to stop the cat like he was catching a fly ball.

Instead, he caught Spooky!

PLOP!

The cat landed in the middle of Cookie's glove! Cookie instinctively swiveled the glove close to his belly, cradling the cat.

Before Cookie could move, Spooky stretched himself straight up the front of Cookie's jersey. Then he gave Cookie's chin a quick lick with his tongue!

"Hey! That tickles!" Cookie said.

But Spooky had already dropped back down into the glove and curled up to sleep.

Cookie stared at the black cat in his glove. "Um, okay, I guess," he said. He looked at Mike and Kate and gave a small shrug. "I gotta get going; we're batting," he said. "I guess I'll take him with me for now. He seems awfully comfortable!"

"I'm sure he's going to bring you good luck, just like 1969!" Kate said.

Cookie's face broke into a big smile. "Sounds good to me," he said. "I'll take care of Spooky. You can stop by after the game."

Whether it was Spooky's good luck, Cookie's confidence, or just great ballplaying, the Mets' luck turned after Spooky made himself at home in their dugout. One Mets batter after another got on base that inning. The fans went wild when Cookie stepped up to the plate.

"Come on, Cookie!" Kate yelled.

"Woo-hoo!" Mike called. He stood up with the other fans to watch Cookie hit.

Cookie didn't disappoint. On the third pitch, he nailed a triple!

The crowd exploded in cheers as two runs scored!

By the time the Mets took the field for the top of the seventh inning, they were ahead by three.

Their winning vibe continued for the rest of the game. The Cubs struggled to come back in the eighth inning by getting one run, but the Mets stayed on top and added two more runs. That meant that at the top of the ninth inning, the Cubs were behind by four.

Three outs later, the game was over. The Mets had won big!

As the stadium cleared, Kate and Mike waited in their seats. Kate messaged her mom to let her know they were going to meet up with Cookie.

"That was an awesome game!" Mike hopped up out of his seat. A ballplayer was waving to them from the field. "I think I see Cookie!"

Mike ran down to the infield railing. Kate followed. But it wasn't Cookie crossing the field to see them.

It was Louie Lopez from the Cubs!

"¡*Hola*!" Louie said as he gave Mike and Kate fist bumps through the safety netting. "What a game that was!"

"It sure was," Kate said. "Sorry you lost!"

Louie waved his hand. "It was exciting.

113

That's all that matters to me," he said. "But I heard you had some excitement, too, with Ash and the black cat. She talked with the Cubs after the game and apologized for trying to get revenge. She's also going to tell the Mets she's sorry and clean up all the cat drawings she made in the stadium."

Before Mike or Kate could respond, a familiar sound crossed their ears.

MEOW! MEOW! MEOW!

Cookie emerged from the nearby Mets' dugout with a familiar cat in his right hand.

"Spooky!" Kate said.

MEOW! Spooky replied.

Cookie stepped up next to Louie and gave him a big side hug. Louie pretended to push him away but then gave him a high five.

"I'll admit you Cubs gave us a scare tonight," Cookie said to Louie. "But we powered back after finding our black cat super-power, thanks to Mike and Kate! You two did an incredible job solving the black cat mystery."

"Thanks, Cookie!" Kate said. She nodded at Spooky. "It looks like you found a new friend."

"You don't mind holding him?" Mike asked. "You had some problems with cats earlier today."

Cookie held Spooky up and rubbed the cat's nose against his. "Oh sure," he said.

"It turns out that after meeting this little guy I'm not afraid of cats anymore!"

"I'd call that a black cat changeup," Louie said. "Nice job!"

Mike, Kate, and Cookie laughed.

"Are you sure you're okay with him, Cookie?" Kate asked. "We could still take him back to the shelter."

"Not a chance!" Cookie said. He petted the top of Spooky's head as the cat tried to lick his hand. "Spooky's not going anywhere. We're planning on taking him all the way to the World Series this year!"

Dugout Notes

New York Mets

The Miracle Mets. In the seven years before 1969, the Mets never had a winning season. They'd never even finished higher than second to last in the National League. But 1969 was different. Although they trailed the Chicago Cubs by ten games in the middle of August, their luck changed. The Mets went on a tear in late August and into September and October. They finished eight games ahead of the Cubs with a 100–62 record and went on to the World Series. The 1969 Mets team is called the Miracle Mets or the Amazin' Mets because they ended up winning the World Series that year, beating the Baltimore Orioles in five games!

Shea Stadium. For their first forty-five years, the Mets played at Shea Stadium. Shea Stadium was located in the Queens section of New York City. It was named after William Shea, a New York lawyer who helped bring the Mets to New York. Shea Stadium also hosted the New York Jets football team until 1984 and the Yankees in 1974–75.

The stadium was torn down in 2009.

Citi Field. The Mets have played at Citi Field since 2009. It replaced Shea Stadium and was built right next door. In fact, there are markers in the Citi Field parking lot for Shea Stadium's old home plate, pitcher's mound, and bases. The main walkway behind the outfield crosses over Shea Bridge, a large metal bridge, which honors the Mets' former stadium. Visitors can stop by the FanFest area behind the center-field scoreboard. It includes a Wiffle ball field, batting cage, and more.

Halloween foul poles. At the Mets' stadium, it's Halloween every day. That's because their foul poles are painted orange instead of yellow! The team painted them orange not to get ready for a scary October holiday but because orange and blue are the team colors.

Tom Seaver. Over the years, the Mets have had lots of great players. But Tom Seaver, number 41, was one of their best. Tom pitched for the Mets from 1967 to 1977 and again in 1983. His nickname was Tom Terrific. He won three Cy Young awards, was a twelve-time All-Star, and won the National League Rookie of the Year award in

1967. He was elected to the National Baseball Hall of Fame, and the Mets retired his number 41.

Fun fans. Although their team doesn't always win, the Mets have some of the most enthusiastic fans in baseball. The 7 Line Army is a group of fans named after the number 7 train that goes from New York City to the stadium. They sit together, wear Mets shirts, and sometimes even "invade" other teams' stadiums to make the Mets feel at home on away games. Cowbell Man is a fan who wears a Mets jersey and plays a cowbell during Mets home games. His cowbell can be heard throughout the stadium!

Bobby Bonilla Day. Even though former MLB player Bobby Bonilla hasn't played for the Mets since 1999, every July 1 he gets a payment from the Mets for $1.2 million! That's why July 1 is known to Mets fans as Bobby Bonilla Day. Instead of paying him $5.9 million in 2000, the team decided to pay him $1.19 million a year plus interest for twenty-five years, starting in 2011. They figured it was a good deal. But it seems like a better deal for Bobby!

Casey Stengel. The first manager of the Mets, Casey Stengel, was previously a manager for the Brooklyn Dodgers, the Boston Braves, and the New York

Yankees. His record for the first season with the Mets was 40 wins and 120 losses! The Mets finished last every year he managed the team. But his team and the fans loved him. Stengel was known for coming up with funny phrases, such as "Good pitching will always stop good hitting and vice-versa."

☆ **About the Author** ☆

DAVID A. KELLY is a former Little League right fielder. These days, he can often be found enjoying a game at a major-league park. He is also the author of the MVP series, *Babe Ruth and the Baseball Curse*, *Miracle Mud*, and *Tee Time on the Moon*. He lives outside of Boston with his family. For more information visit davidakellybooks.com. Author school or library visits available at dakvisits.com.

Printed in the USA
CPSIA information can be obtained
at www.ICGtesting.com
CBHW060217060824
12764CB00011B/640